MOG'S
Amazing Birthday
Caper

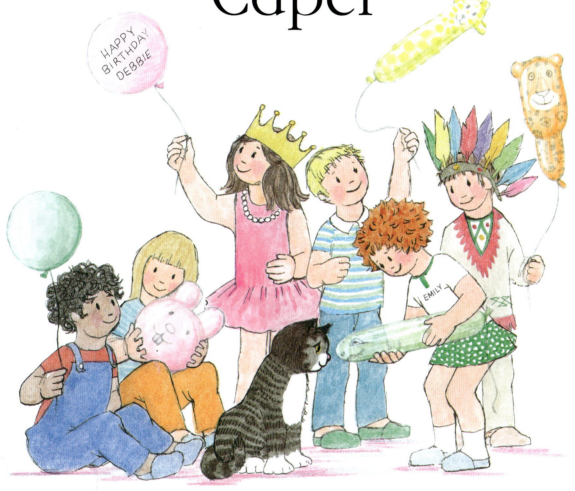

written and illustrated by

Judith Kerr

HarperCollins *Children's Books*

For Tom, Tacy and Matthew

Other books by Judith Kerr include:

Mog's Christmas	Mog and the V.E.T.
Mog and the Baby	Mog's Bad Thing
Mog in the Dark	Goodbye Mog
Mog the Forgetful Cat	Birdie Halleluyah!
Mog and Bunny	The Tiger Who Came to Tea
Mog and Barnaby	The Other Goose
Mog on Fox Night	Goose in a Hole
Mog and the Granny	

First published in hardback in Great Britain by William Collins Sons & Co. Ltd in 1986. First published in paperback by Picture Lions in 1989. Re-issued by HarperCollins Children's Books in 2005. First published as *Mog's ABC* by HarperCollins Children's Books in 2007

11

ISBN-13: 978-0-00-717131-6

Visit our website at: www.harpercollins.co.uk
Printed and bound in China

Aa

Mog accidentally ate an alligator
and all were amazed at the…

...BANG!

Bb

Boohoo!

Biting balloons is bad !
Bursting birthday balloons
is beastly !

"You clumsy cat! You crushed the cake and candles!"

Mog creeps off…

Cc

crossly…   to a corner…   for a catnap.

Dd

She dreams and dreams and dreams.
She dreams of dragons doing damage in the dark…

...and elephants eating Emily...

Ee

Ff

...and her family floating far into a fog.

Gg

Goodness! A giraffe in the garden.

Hh

Mog
hisses
and
he
hops
into
a
helicopter.

I i

"May I invite you to an ice cream?"
inquires an Indian.

Jj

A jaguar joins them with a jug of jelly…

Kk

...to eat with a kipper and ketchup from the kettle.

Ll

But look who is lurking!
Lying low! Licking lips! It's…

Mm

A monster!

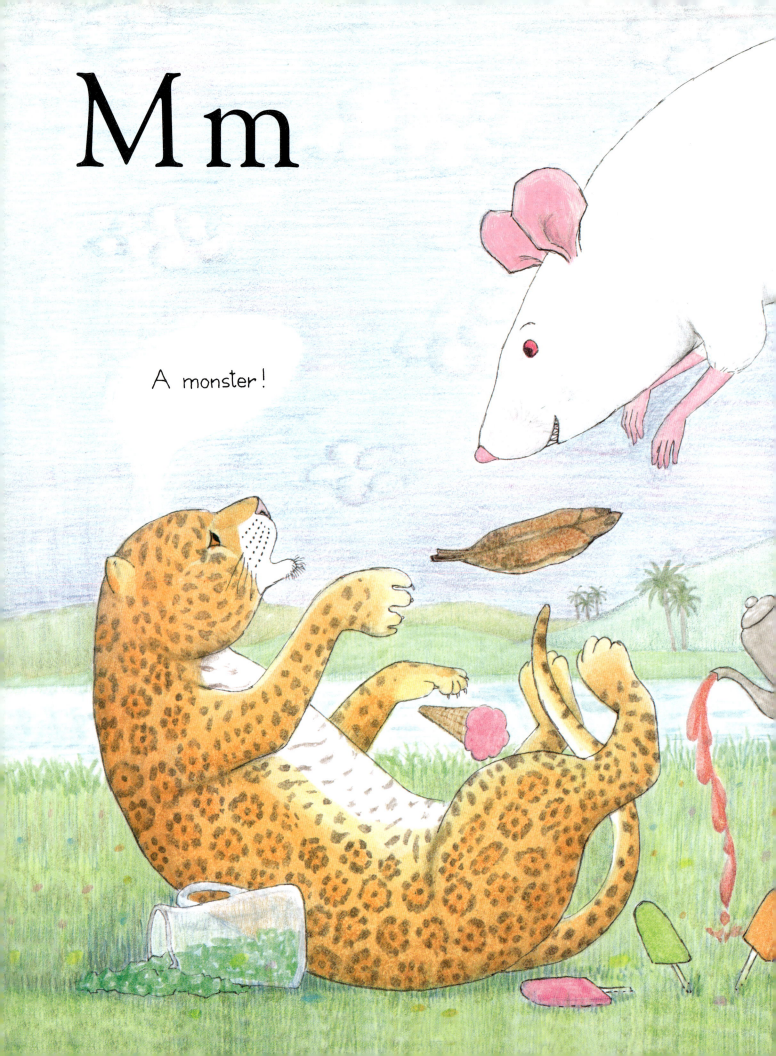

Nn

"Don't nip my nose, you nightmare nibbler!"

It has not noticed Nicky with his net.

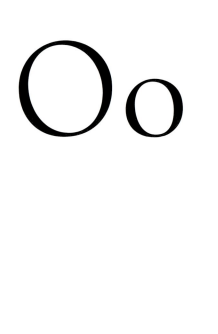

Oo

Oh! Ooh! Oops!

Outwitted!

Outraged!

Overpowered!

Pp

Mog purrs, and they paddle past palm trees and parrots to a pale pink palace with purple pillars.

Qq

But what is that queer quiver?
A quake! An earthquake!
"I feel quite queasy," says the queen.

Rr

The raging river rises round them.
"Run!" she roars. "My royal rug will rescue us."

Ss

Soaring into the sky, Mog sees survivors struggling on a sinking sofa, surrounded by smiling sharks.

Tt

They're terrified!
They're Mr and Mrs Thomas!
They teeter, totter, trip,
their treacherous transport tilts…

Uu

Unbalanced!

Upset!

Upended!

Underwater

Vv

But on the verge of vanishing for ever,
Mog hears a voice,
first vague, then very vivid…

W w

"Why are your whiskers wet?
What is this water?
Wake up! We're on our way
to somewhere wonderful!"

X x

Mog goes on an extremely

She examines an axolotl…

exciting expedition.

and exclaims at an ox.

She yawns at a yak,
and then – yippee! Yummy!…

Z z

Out of the zigzag zip-bag zooms something to guzzle,

PICNIC ZONE

and to dazzle and to puzzle the zebras at the zoo.